*To my mother, Sophie,
whose strength and courage
keep me going
K.W.-M.*

Consultants: Said el-Ghithy, Centre for
African Language Lear....g, London, and
Justin Willis, African Studies Centre,
University of Cambridge.

ISBN: 0-7868-0552-8 (trade)

First Edition

1 3 5 7 9 10 8 6 4 2

Printed in China

Full Library of Congress Publication data on file.

Furaha Means Happy

A Book of Swahili Words

Written and illustrated by
Ken Wilson-Max

Jump at the Sun

Hyperion Books for Children
New York

Africa

Africa is a big continent where many people live. Kenya (*Ken*-yer) is one of its many countries. You can see it shaded in yellow on this map.

Wambui (Wom-*boo*-ee) and her brother, Moses, live in Kenya. They speak English and Swahili (Swuh-*hee*-lee), a language that is spoken all over East Africa and is the main language of Kenya. As you play along with Wambui and Moses, you can learn some Swahili words. The pronunciation guide in the back of the book will help you make the sounds of the words.

Kenya

Moses   Wambui

Hello! My name is Wambui.
Today my mom and dad
took my brother and me for a trip
to the lake. Our dog came along, too.

On the way, we stopped the car to
watch two giraffes nibbling leaves
from the tops of trees.

Dad **Baba**

Mom **Mama**

Dog **Mbwa**

Car **Gari**

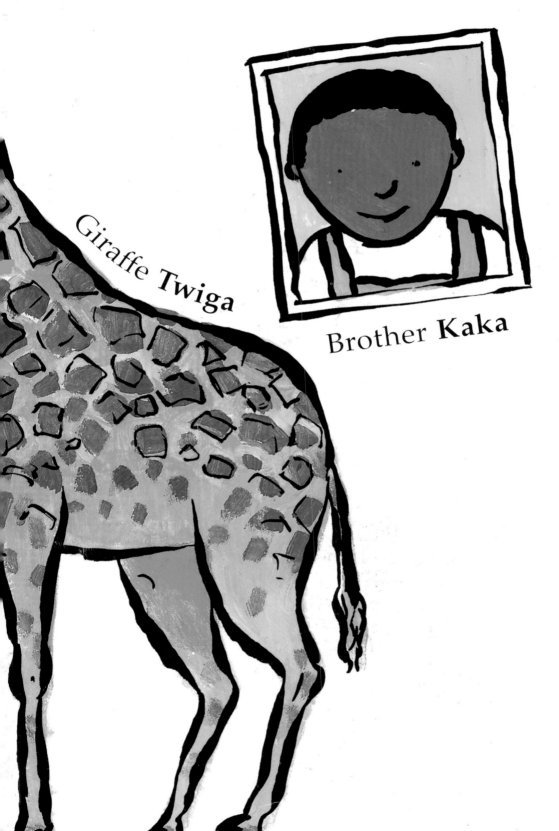

Giraffe **Twiga**

Brother **Kaka**

When we got to the lake, we went for a walk. I put on my hat and carried my bucket and shovel.

Everything we needed
for our picnic was in
the basket, and Mom
carried the blanket.

Basket **Kikapu**

Bucket **Ndoo**

Shovel **Sepeto**

Hat **Kofia**

Blanket **Blangeti**

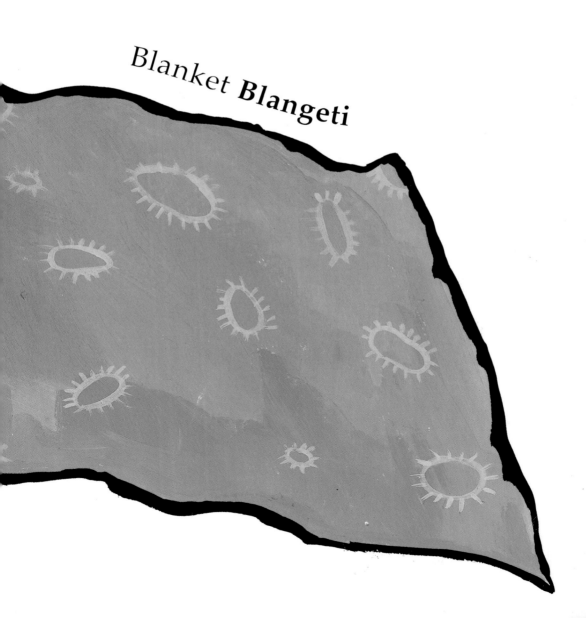

Moses smelled the flowers and looked
for pretty pebbles. We watched hippos
bathing in the lake.

I asked Dad if I could go say hello to them, but he said that hippos don't like it when people get too close. So we left them to have fun on their own.

Hippo **Kiboko**

Lake **Ziwa**

Pebbles **Kokoto**

Flower **Ua**

After we found the perfect place for our picnic, we sat down, ate a plate of sandwiches, and drank juice. Moses and I finished our meal with some delicious, ripe mangoes.

But mangoes are messy—the
juice dripped all over our clothes!

Sandwich **Sanguwichi**

Clothes **Nguo**

Plate Sahani

Juice Maji ya matunda

Mango Embe

After lunch, we dozed in the shade
of a large tree. I rested my head on
a pillow, and Mom took a picture of
me with her camera.

Our dog lay on the grass and chewed
his stick. We all had a very happy day!

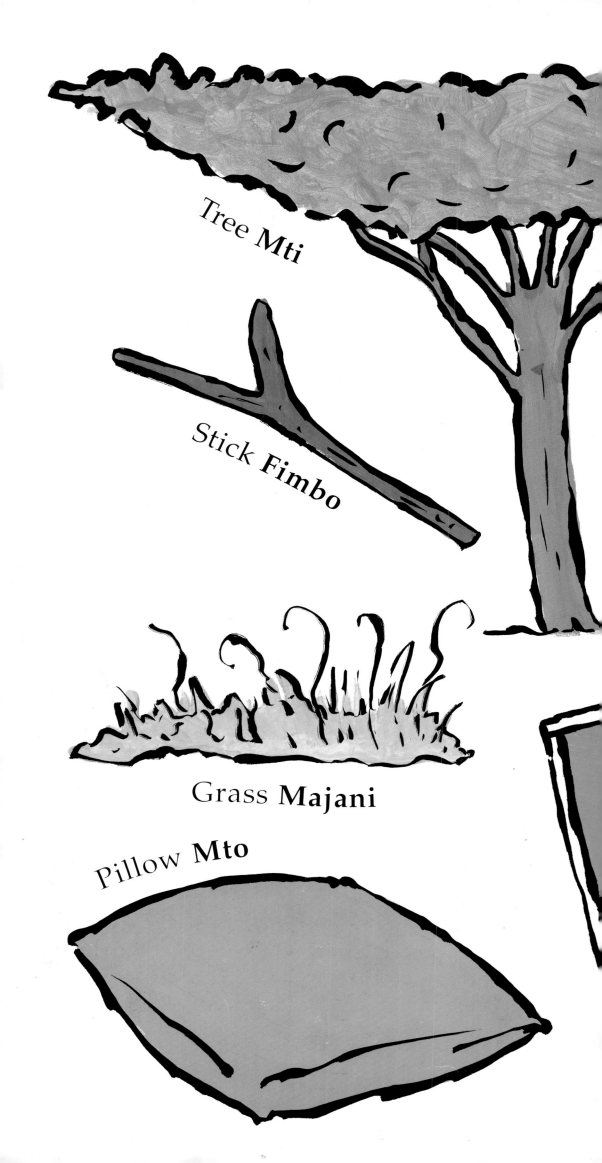

Tree **Mti**

Stick **Fimbo**

Grass **Majani**

Pillow **Mto**

Camera Kamera

Picture Picha

How to Say the Words

All the words in this book are easy to say if you split the words into single parts. These parts are called syllables. Each syllable has its own sound. Some syllables are called stressed syllables. These are the syllables shown in italics in the word list you see. They are louder and longer than unstressed syllables.

In unstressed syllables, the vowels **a, e, i, o** and **u** sound like this: **a** as in sugar, **e** as in bed, **i** as in bit, **o** as in born and **u** as in full. In stressed syllables, they sound like this: **a** as in father, **e** as in reign, **i** as in piece, **o** as in boat, and **u** as in rule.

Learning new words in any language takes time and practice. Ask an adult to help you, and have fun!

A happy day....... *Si*-ku ya fu-*ra*-ha
Basket.................. Ki-*ka*-pu
Blanket.............. Blan-*ge*-ti
Brother.............. *Ka*-ka
Bucket.............. N-*do*-o
Camera.............. Ka-*me*-ra
Car.................... *Ga*-ri
Clothes.............. *Ngu*-o
Dad.................... *Ba*-ba
Dog.................... M-bwa
Flower.............. *U*-a
Giraffe.............. *Twi*-ga
Grass.................. Ma-*ja*-ni
Hat.................... Ko-*fi*-a
Hippo................ Ki-*bo*-ko
Juice.................. *Ma*-ji ya ma-*tun*-da
Lake.................. *Zi*-wa
Mango................ *Em*-be
Mom.................. *Ma*-ma
Pebbles.............. Ko-*ko*-to
Picture.............. *Pi*-cha
Pillow................ M-*to*
Plate.................. Sa-*ha*-ni
Sandwich.......... Sang-u-*wi*-chi
Shovel................ Se-*pe*-to
Stick.................. *Fim*-bo
Tree.................. M-*ti*